W9-ABM-800

A REALLY NEW SCHOOL

An Up2U Action Adventure

magic wagon

By: Jan Fields

Illustrated by: Vivienne To

visit us at www.abdopublishing.com

Printed in the United States of America, North Mankato, Minnesota.
052013
092013
 This book contains at least 10% recycled materials.

Written by Jan Fields
Illustrated by Vivienne To
Edited by Stephanie Hedlund and Rochelle Baltzer
Cover and interior design by Neil Klinepier

Library of Congress Cataloging-in-Publication Data

Fields, Jan.
  A really new school : an Up2U action adventure / by Jan Fields ;
illustrated by Vivienne To.
     p. cm. -- (Up2U adventures)
  Summary: Ana thinks that her new elementary school is very
strange, and when she and her new friend Bryce discover a secret
passage they know that something suspicious is going on, but it is up
to the reader to decide whether the school is a secret training ground,
an illegal experiment, or something else.
  ISBN 978-1-61641-969-1
1. Plot-your-own stories. 2. Elementary schools--Juvenile fiction.
3. Adventure stories. [1. Secrets--Fiction. 2. Elementary schools--
Fiction. 3. Schools--Fiction. 4. Adventure and adventurers--Fiction.]
I. To, Vivienne, ill. II. Title.
  PZ7.F479177Re 2013
  813.6--dc23
                        2013001731

TABLE OF CONTENTS

SCARED?

Ana shrugged out of her tan jacket and hung it on the peg in the narrow locker. She hung her tan backpack on the peg above the jacket. Once everything was hung up, she put her brown paper lunch bag on the floor of the locker. Each item looked and sat exactly according to the rules.

All up and down the row of lockers, other kids did exactly the same thing in exactly the same way. The strange thing was, that none of the lockers had doors. And none had any personal touches or decorations. Everything looked exactly the same.

"Our lockers don't need doors," Principal Carson had told Ana when she asked. "Students here have no secrets."

"But what if someone walks off with my jacket or my lunch?" Ana asked.

The principal looked startled. "Stealing is against the rules," he declared.

Middlehurst Elementary School had a lot of rules. And everyone followed them. It was very strange.

Ana's parents thought the new school was great. "You've never had a problem with rules," her dad said. "I don't think that will be a problem at this school. And just think, class time won't be wasted on the kids who goof off."

That was true. But it was also a little spooky. Each day seemed stranger and stranger. No one passed notes. No one kicked the back of her seat. No one whispered. Everyone sat up straight in their seats and stared at the teacher.

In the month Ana had been in school, no one teased her. No one pushed her. No one commented on her thick glasses. And no one offered to be her friend.

Ana glanced toward the restroom doors. She knew she shouldn't have had a second glass of orange juice for breakfast. If she went now, she'd be late for class. No one was ever late for class. It was against the rules. But she really, really had to go.

"Guess I'll be a rule breaker after all," she whispered. Then she walked fast to the bathroom. She hurried, but it was no use. The bell rang as she was washing her hands.

Ana dried her hands quickly using only one paper towel. One paper towel was another rule. Then she peeked out of the bathroom door. The hall was empty except for a boy drinking from the water fountain.

Ana stared at him. "You're late for class," she whispered.

The boy grinned and whispered back, "So are you."

Ana slipped out of the bathroom and walked toward the boy. It surprised her that he didn't sound worried at all. Everyone here seemed worried about breaking the rules.

"Being late is against the rules," Ana announced. "Aren't you scared?"

The boy shrugged. "Everything is against the rules. I overslept, and my mom had to drive me. No big deal."

Ana thought it was a really big deal. After all, everything that wasn't perfect was a really big deal here. Just as she was wondering if the boy was actually a student at Middlehurst, he pointed down the hall.

"Look at that," he demanded.

Ana turned to look at what he was pointing toward. When she turned, all she saw was a row of lockers with no doors. It looked just like every other wall in the school.

"Yeah? It's lockers. What about them?" she asked.

The boy just shook his head at her. He turned and jogged toward the lockers. At the end of the row, he shoved his hand into a dark crack where the lockers met the wall.

"Don't you see? This crack leads somewhere. Help me pull," he demanded.

"That's got to be against the rules," Ana muttered. But she walked over to help.

Together they slowly swung the lockers away from the wall. The opening revealed a hallway behind the lockers that extended into the dark. The boy turned and grinned at her.

"We just found a secret passage in our school," he whispered. "How cool is that? Let's find out where it goes."

Ana peered into the darkness. "Are you out of your mind? I'm getting to class," she said, turning on her heel to leave.

The boy tugged at her uniform sleeve. "Come on," he said. "You're already late. Let's have some fun for a change. You're not scared, are you?"

"Of course I'm scared," Ana said. But she was also curious. This school seemed so perfect, and now this. She had to know what was hidden in the hall. She took a deep breath and finally said, "Okay, let's go."

HIDDEN PASSAGES

As soon as they stepped into the passage, the boy started pulling on the wall of lockers. "What are you doing?" Ana demanded.

"I don't want some teacher catching us," he answered. "We need to pull it back to a crack."

"Oh, good idea." Ana watched the lockers swing toward them. She thought he was pulling a little too hard. Suddenly, the lockers snapped into place with no crack of light showing.

"Oops," the boy said.

Now that their way out was blocked, Ana was frightened. She pushed against the wall of lockers.

"Help me get this back open," she whispered.

She felt the boy move next to her. They both pushed hard, but the wall didn't move.

"Great," she said. "Now we're trapped."

"I guess we'll have to see where this goes," the boy said. He grabbed her arm and began pulling her down the dark passage.

"We're in so much trouble," Ana moaned as she stumbled along. Her eyes were slowly adjusting to the darkness. Now the boy looked like a shadowy blob. "And I don't even know your name."

"My name is Bryce," he said cheerfully. "And you're Ana."

"How do you know that?" she asked. "We've never met before."

"I was the new kid before you," he told her. "And then you came. Before your first day, they told everyone your name. They told us all about you before you started."

"Oh." Ana said in shock. *No wonder no one has asked my name*, she thought.

She plodded along in the dark for a few moments. As she walked, she trailed her hand along the wall so she could stay in a straight line. She was afraid she'd bounce from wall to wall otherwise.

"How new are you?" she asked finally.

"I've been here two months and three detentions." His shadowy blob shook a little as he laughed at his own joke.

"Have you made any friends?" she asked. She figured he probably had. At her old school, kids liked boys like him.

"Are you kidding?" he asked. "Among the robo-students? I think they're afraid they'll catch detention germs. I bet they love you though."

"Not so much," she said quietly.

Suddenly, they heard a rustle and a scrape from just ahead. They both froze. When nothing else happened, they crept slowly down the hallway. Soon, they ran into a wall.

"Do you think this is a blank wall?" Bryce asked.

"Maybe," Ana said. "Or maybe the hall turns. We need to feel for the other walls." She saw the shadowy Bryce blob move to the left. She went the other way and felt along for the right wall. She found nothing but open space.

"The tunnel continues this way," she whispered.

"It goes this way, too," he whispered back. "Which way do we go?"

Ana tried to imagine how the strange hallway fit in with the layout of the school. She was pretty sure that going left would take them farther away from the office. That had to be a good idea. She certainly didn't want to come to the end of the hall and find it opened into the principal's office.

"Let's go left," she said, turning to follow the dark shadow of Bryce. Since Bryce was all the way across the hall from her, he stayed in front as they walked. Ana considered hurrying to catch up with him. She liked the idea of having someone to grab if something scared her. Still, she didn't want to look like a baby. Or worse, he might think she actually liked him.

"Shouldn't the school look a lot bigger on the outside?" Ana asked after they had walked a short while. "I mean, it has to be bigger if it has hidden tunnels and all."

"I was just wondering that my- . . . hey!" Bryce's yelp turned into a shriek. Ana heard thumps and more than one "ouch." The dark shadowy blob of Bryce had disappeared completely.

"Bryce?" Ana whispered as loud as she dared. She slowly crept forward, not sure what happened to Bryce. She slid her foot carefully along the floor.

"Bryce?" she called out again, a little louder than the last time.

Only silence answered her.

EXPLORING

As Ana edged forward by inches, she kept calling for Bryce. Still no answer. She moved faster, fighting the panicky urge to turn around and run. Her left foot slid quickly across the floor. Everything felt solid. Then, her right foot slid into empty air.

Ana yelped, throwing herself backward away from the drop-off. She landed on her behind with a thud. Her heart pounded. She began scooting once again toward the drop-off, but she stayed sitting. That way, she could reach ahead with her feet and not worry about falling.

When she felt the edge of the drop-off, she scooted closer. She reached over the edge carefully, feeling with her toes. She struck a ledge almost immediately. It was fairly narrow.

She scooted until she was as close to the edge as she dared. She felt past the ledge with her toes. She felt another ledge.

"Stairs," she whispered. Bryce had fallen down a set of stairs. Ana began scooting down the stairs one by one until her foot nudged something soft. Ana scooted closer and reached out. She felt shirt, arm, and hair. "Bryce!"

"Shhhh," Bryce hissed. "I heard something in the hall down there." She felt his arm move under her hand as he pointed ahead. "So I'm trying to be quiet and hide."

"Screaming as you fell down the stairs was probably a good start," Ana said.

"Hey!" he said. "You try falling down a set of stairs without yelling."

"You scared me to death," Ana complained. "Are you hurt?"

"My arm hurts a little," Bryce admitted. "And my knee kind of hurts, too. Nothing serious. I just need to be more careful."

"What we need," Ana said, "is some light."

Just as she said that, lights snapped on up and down the hallway. "That can't be good," Bryce muttered.

Ana crept up the stairs and peeked over the top. She could see back to where the hall they'd entered formed a T. The physical education teacher and Principal Carson walked out where Ana could see them. She ducked lower on the steps.

"Turn right, turn right, turn right," she mouthed.

She heard the adults' footsteps moving farther away and dared another peek. The two men were walking down the right-hand hall, away from Ana and Bryce. The flood of relief made Ana feel a little shaky. She slipped back down the stairs.

"It was Coach King and Principal Carson," she whispered. "They probably turned on the lights. We should get out of here before the lights go off again."

"I'm all for that," Bryce said. He scrambled to his feet. He started walking down the hall away from the stairs.

"Where are you going?" Ana asked. "I meant we should go back out the way we came."

"You really think they left the lockers open again?" Bryce asked. "They're closed for sure now."

"But with the lights on, we can probably see how to get them back open," she insisted.

"Unless the lights go out just as we get there," Bryce reasoned. He shook his head. "I'm going this way."

Ana looked down the hallway. She noticed that it slanted downward. It looked like it was headed underground. Something about that made her very nervous.

"Really, I think we should go back," she said.

"Go back then," Bryce said, turning and starting down the hall again. "I'll see you later."

Ana felt like screaming with frustration. She didn't want to go deeper underground. But she didn't want to find herself trapped in the dark all alone. She weighed the two rotten choices and finally trotted to catch up with Bryce.

When she caught up with him, he didn't say a word. But he definitely looked a little smug. They hurried down the hall together. It not only sloped downward, but it also curved slightly left.

With the soft lighting from the ceiling, they could see that the walls weren't as smooth as they thought. The outlines of doors were clear on the right-hand wall, but none of the doors had handles. Bryce stopped in front of one and began pressing at random spots on the door.

"How do you think these open?"

Ana shrugged then she leaned in close to look at the door. Suddenly a beam of light flashed right into her eye. She jumped back so fast that she fell down.

"What was that?" she asked.

"I don't know," Bryce said. "It came right off the door. Did it hurt?"

"No," she said. "And I can see okay. It was weird."

"Everything about this school is weird," Bryce said. He held out his hand to help Ana up. "We better keep going."

As she trotted down the hall, Ana kept blinking. Why did the door do that? Maybe if she'd done something different, the door would have opened. She was still wondering what the light was when they turned a corner and almost ran right into a blank wall.

This time there was no passage leading off to either side. It was just a wall. They'd hit a dead end.

"I guess we'll have to go all the way back and try the right-hand passage," Bryce said.

As they turned around, they both froze. They heard the faint sound of voices in the hall. Someone was coming their way. They were trapped!

A SECRET ROOM

Ana turned toward the dead end and ran her hands over the smooth surface. She saw that the edge where the wall met the corridor showed a clear crack.

"I think this is a door," she whispered.

"Great," Bryce said. "If we could open it."

Ana put her face close to the wall, peering at the smooth surface near the right edge. Just as before, a beam of light appeared and flashed into her eye. Ana held still and tried not to blink.

"Don't hurt me," she murmured.

The light flashed off and the wall began to move, swinging inward.

"Way to go, Ana," Bryce whispered.

They squeezed through the open door. Once inside, they quickly threw themselves against it. It slowly swung closed.

"Now we hide," Ana said.

They turned and looked at the large room they'd entered. It was about the size of the school's gym and looked a lot like it. The floor was glossy wood and thick mats were leaning against the walls.

As they walked toward the rear of the room, Ana saw racks with body pads. They looked like protective gear she'd seen football players or martial artists wear. Also on the rack were poles and wooden swords. A small table held tools and various other things, some Ana couldn't even guess at what they might be.

"Weird gym," Bryce said. "There aren't a lot of hiding places."

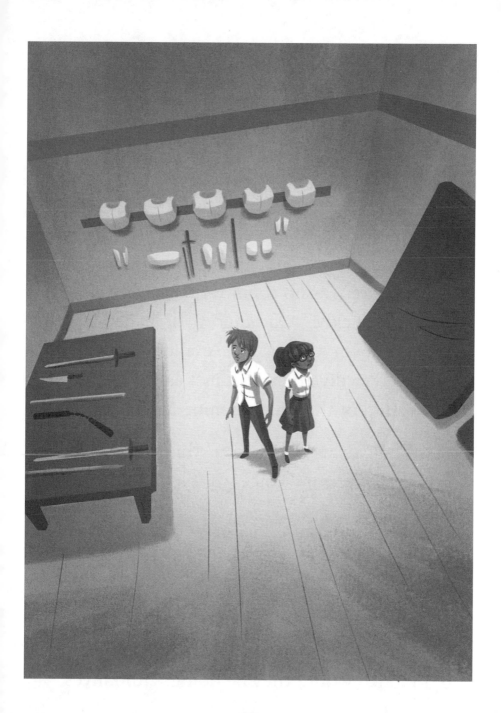

Ana pointed toward a spot where two thick mats leaned against the wall. She trotted toward them. "I think we can squeeze behind those."

"It's going to be tight," Bryce said.

It was. Ana let Bryce go first since he was bigger. Once he had squeezed into the small space, there was no room for Ana. She looked around quickly. Another pad leaned alone farther down the wall. Ana ran for it and managed to dive behind it just as she heard the soft sound of the door opening again.

"What exactly do you think we need?" Principal Carson's voice was clear and seemed scary close.

"I think it's time we began practicing with knives," Coach King said. "They're more practical."

Ana's eyes grew round. Knives? What kind of practice would they be doing with knives?

"I'm not sure I see why that's practical," Principal Carson said.

"That's because you haven't seen my new invention," Coach King replied.

The two voices grew a bit fainter. Ana knew they must have walked toward the far wall. She carefully inched toward the opening of the mat. She caught sight of the two adults. They were facing one of the racks that lined the back wall.

Coach King picked up a jacket that hung from the end of the rack. He quickly slipped into the jacket. "Search me," he said.

Principal Carson quickly patted the coach down. It looked like the searches on every police show Ana had ever seen.

"Find anything?" Coach King asked.

"No," the principal said. "Are you telling me you've hidden something that I can't feel?"

"Absolutely." Coach King walked to the center of the room and Ana slipped deeper behind the mat. "Now watch this."

Suddenly something thumped into the mat Ana was hiding behind. She squeaked slightly in surprise. Then, she clamped her hand over her mouth.

"Did you hear something?" Principal Carson asked.

"Only the sound of my success. Come on, admit it. This is a great idea. The blades are hidden from searches, but they can be grabbed in a second."

"Yes, you were great," the principal said. "But I'm sure I heard something."

"The mat shifted," Coach King said. "Or we have a mouse. Don't change the subject. It's time to expand our training. Watch this."

Ana tightened her hand over her mouth to keep from shrieking. Three more thumps shook the mat hiding her.

"Okay, I'll think about it," the principal said. "Now, stop damaging the mats."

"Do you want to put in some sparring time?" Coach King asked. "You don't want to get soft."

"I don't have time right now," the principal said. "I have some parents coming in. Apparently, we have a couple of students who skipped school today."

"Middlehurst students?" Coach King asked, sounding shocked.

"Don't worry," Principal Carson said. "When we catch them, they'll never try it again."

Ana froze as the two adults left the room. A couple of kids who skipped school? She scrambled out from behind the mat and pointed at Bryce.

"They were talking about us!" she said. "My parents are going to be so mad!"

Bryce grinned at her. "Then I guess you shouldn't have skipped school."

"I didn't," Ana insisted. "I'm in school. In fact, I'm trapped in school." She put her head in her hands and moaned. What was she going to do now?

"We just have to keep looking for a way out," Bryce said. "And I think having angry parents is the least of our problems."

"How can you say that?" Ana asked.

Bryce pointed over Ana's shoulder. She turned around and looked at the leaning mats. Four knife blades were buried about halfway in the soft foam of the mat.

"Oh no," Ana said. "What kind of place is this?"

"All I know," Bryce said as he peered closely at the blades, "is that this school is much cooler than I thought. I thought they were just creating robo-students, not action heroes. This is awesome!"

"No, it's not," Ana insisted. "Cool teachers don't practice knife throwing in their spare time."

"Do you think we should take some of them with us?" he asked. "Just in case."

"No, no, we shouldn't," Ana said. "Knives are sharp and scary and you could cut your finger off."

Bryce looked at her. "You sound like my mom."

"Well, excuse me for being careful," Ana snapped. "The last time I did something crazy, I ended up trapped in creepy tunnels."

Bryce shrugged. "It beats playing the 'who looks suspicious' game. Especially when the teacher gets to throw erasers at you if you pick the wrong person. Last time I got home after that lesson, my mom wanted to know why I had white streaks in my hair."

"I'm better at that one than at electrical wiring," Ana said. "I got shocked twice last week. Anyway, that doesn't matter. We have to get out of here."

"Fine," he said. "We could go back toward the office in the other tunnel. It might let us out in a hall." Then his eyes lit up. "There's a janitor's closet near the office. We could pretend we got locked in. That would mean we didn't skip school."

"Why would we be in a janitor's closet?" Ana asked. "And how exactly did we get locked in it anyway?"

"We'll figure that out when we get there," Bryce replied. "Now, we need to get moving while that light stays on in the hallway." He grabbed Ana's arm and began towing her toward the door. In the brightly lit room, it was easy to see how to open the door.

Unfortunately, once they opened it, they saw the hall was pitch black again.

"Oh, no," Ana said. "We're too late. I really don't want to creep around in the dark anymore."

With the room light shining in the hall, Bryce spotted a switch on the wall. "We can just turn on the lights!"

As he reached for the switch, Ana grabbed his arm. "No, don't!"

He looked at her in surprise. "Why not?"

"What if they come into the hall again and find the lights on," she said. "They'll know we were in here."

"So what do you want to do?" Bryce asked. "Do you want to wander in the dark again or turn on the light? Those seem like the only two options to me."

Suddenly Ana smiled. "I have an idea."

RUN!

Ana turned and raced back to the table she'd seen earlier. Among the tools and strange bits, she found a small flashlight.

"Please work, please work," she muttered as she pressed the button. The light seemed tiny in the big, brightly lit room, but she knew it would help in the tunnel.

When she ran back to the door, Bryce frowned. "You couldn't find two?"

"I'm happy I found one," she said. "Now let's find our way out of here."

The hall was spookier with just the small flashlight's beam. Shadows pooled near the walls and stretched around corners. As they passed each smooth door, Bryce paused longer and longer.

"Come on," Ana said. "We need to get to that janitor's closet."

"Yeah, I remember," he said. "But now that you know the light thing shining in your eye opens the doors, don't you want to know what's in there?"

"Not particularly," she said. But she slowed down and stared at the next door when Bryce did.

"We could take a peek into one of them," he said.

She knew it was a bad idea. But curiosity seemed to root her to the hallway floor. "Maybe just a peek to find out what is going on," she said. "But use your eye this time."

Bryce leaned close to the door. A beam of light shone out and hit his eye. He blinked but didn't back away. Eventually, the door slid smoothly into the wall on the right side.

The room they faced looked like a small bedroom with a single bed, a small dresser, and a mirror. A boy about their age jumped up from the bed and stood straight and still.

"Who are you?" Bryce asked.

The boy's head snapped toward them and his whole body relaxed. "I'm Connor. Who are you?" he asked.

"I'm Bryce," Bryce said before Ana could shush him. She wasn't sure it was smart to give their names to some strange kid. What if he told on them?

"How come you're out of your room?" Connor asked.

"We don't have rooms here," Bryce said. "We just go to school and then go home. I didn't know kids lived here."

The kid grunted. "It's not like I had a choice. Hey, do they know you guys are back here?"

Bryce and Ana looked at each other. It was like they silently agreed to tell this stranger the truth. Slowly, they shook their heads.

Connor stared at them, open-mouthed. "You two are going to be in so much trouble," he sputtered.

"We already are," Ana said. "Principal Carson called our parents."

Connor laughed, but he didn't sound happy. "Skipping school is bad. You'll get detention for sure. But being caught back here, that's really bad. You guys have got to get out of here."

"Do you know how?" Ana said. "We came in where a row of lockers were hiding a door, but it swung shut and we were trapped. We thought maybe one of the tunnels came out near the office."

"It does," Connor said as he stepped out of the room. "I can show you. Maybe I can even get away." His voice sounded thick and funny when he talked about getting away.

"How long have you been in here?" Ana asked.

Connor turned and touched the wall beside the open door. The door slipped shut silently. "Since the first week of school," he answered. "I really miss my folks . . . and my dog. And sometimes even my baby brother."

The three walked down the hall in silence. Ana glanced at the other doors. Was there a kid behind every one of them? Should they get them all out? She knew it would be a lot harder to sneak a whole bunch of kids out. Finally, she decided they should get out now, but bring their parents back later to free the other kids.

With the flashlight, they could move quickly through the halls and dash up the stairs. They were soon at the spot where the hallways formed a T.

"Should we go back out the way we came in?" Ana whispered.

"Not if we're going to try saying we were stuck in the janitor's closet," Bryce said.

"And it'll be easier for me to get away if I can get out the front doors," Connor added. "They're close to where the other tunnel ends."

Ana nodded. She handed the flashlight to Connor. "Since you know the way, you should lead."

"Okay." Connor hurried down the hallway. Ana saw more doors along the new tunnel. Unlike the tunnel they'd left, this one stayed level. It was shorter than the other tunnel as well. They quickly came to what seemed like a dead end.

Connor swept the flashlight along the wall. In the dim beam of light, Ana didn't see anything unusual. She hoped Connor knew what he was doing. Finally, the sweeping light stopped and the boy reached out and pushed at the wall. It immediately swung outward. Bright light from the school hallway poured in.

Blinking from light blindness, they stumbled out into the school hallway. The door swung closed behind them and Ana saw that it was completely hidden by a tall trophy case.

They looked up and down the empty hall. "Thanks for getting me out," Connor said.

"Thanks for getting *us* out," Bryce answered.

Connor headed for the front door as Bryce tugged on Ana's sleeve. He pointed toward the janitor's closet. Suddenly the door to the school office opened. All three kids froze as Coach King stepped out and said, "Connor?"

Connor stood straight and tall. He pointed at Ana and Bryce and said, "I found these two in the tunnel. I was coming to report."

Coach King turned to look at Ana and Bryce. He smiled. It wasn't a very nice smile. "So you found our missing students. Very good."

Ana couldn't believe Connor had betrayed them like that. She backed away from Coach King and ran into Bryce. "Run!" Bryce said.

But before they could spin around to run, a hand clamped down on each of their shoulders. "No running in the halls," Principal Carson said. "It's a rule. And you know how important rules are here at Middlehurst Elementary School."

"I want to talk to my parents," Ana insisted.

"I'm afraid that won't be possible," Principal Carson said. "Your parents just left. They were so worried. It's not like you to run away, Ana. You normally follow the rules so well."

The principal looked at Bryce and smiled. "Your mother was much less shocked."

"So call them back," Bryce said.

"You are not in a position to give orders," Principal Carson said. "Right now, we're going someplace quiet to talk about your punishment."

Principal Carson began dragging Ana and Bryce toward the trophy case. Bryce kicked the principal hard and screamed, "Fire! Fire! Somebody help!"

The principal let go of Ana and slapped a hand over Bryce's mouth. At the same time, he tried to hold the squirming boy out of kicking range. Suddenly free, Ana spun and raced away.

"Grab her," the principal snapped at Coach King.

Ana could hear the coach's heavy footsteps behind her as she ran. She knew the coach would catch up to her soon. He was taller and ran with longer strides. Just as he sounded close enough to grab her, she crouched down. Coach King couldn't stop in time. He stumbled over

her, sprawling on the floor in front of a row of lockers.

Ana was on her feet in a second, racing in the opposite direction. She saw Connor holding the trophy case door open as the principal dragged Bryce toward it. All of them had their backs to her, so Ana ran as fast as she could and slammed into the back of Principal Carson. He stumbled and let go of Bryce.

Ana grabbed Bryce's hand and raced toward the front door.

Connor stepped in front of them. "You can't get out this way," he whispered. "There's someone outside. Trust me and I'll get you out of here . . ."

THE ENDING IS UP2U!

If you think Ana and Bryce dodge around Connor and go through the door, keep reading on page 50.

If you think Ana and Bryce trust Connor, go to page 60.

But if you want Ana and Bryce to demand Connor tell them what is going on, go to page 69.

ENDING 1: CAUGHT!

"Like we'd believe you," Bryce said, pushing past Connor and hurrying toward the door.

Ana glanced at Connor. She shrugged but followed Bryce. As they reached the door, it swung sharply open. A tall man stepped through, grabbing each of them. Ana recognized him. Sometimes she saw him trimming bushes or mowing grass around the school.

"Looks like you have a little problem, Principal," the man said.

"Bring them here," Principal Carson said as he stood up and dusted off his clothes. "We need to get them out of the hall before the lunch bell rings."

"No problem." The tall man dragged them both down the hall with little effort. They were soon back in the secret hallway. Principal Carson turned on the light.

"Where do you want them?" the man asked.

"Tie them up in one of the storerooms," the principal said. "I'll decide what to do next after school is over. They're either going to be new recruits to welcome or problems to eliminate."

Ana felt her stomach knot up. She had a feeling that they'd get a lot worse than detention if the principal decided they were a problem.

"What is this place?" she asked, her voice high and quivering.

"It's a school," the principal said. "Haven't you been paying attention, girl?"

"It's more than just a school," Bryce said. "Schools don't have secret panels and prisoners. We want to know what is going on here."

"Maybe you just haven't been going to the right schools," the tall man said. He laughed loudly at his own joke.

Finally they stopped. The principal leaned close to a door so the light could flash on his eye. When the door opened, the tall man dragged Bryce and Ana inside. Connor followed them all in silently.

The principal picked up a roll of duct tape from a pile of shipping boxes. As the tall man held Bryce and Ana back to back, the principal wrapped the tape around and around them. Then the tall man pushed them down to sit on the floor and the principal taped their ankles.

"That should keep you still," the principal said. "Now to keep you quiet." He stuck another piece of tape over their mouths.

"I'll see you in a few hours," the principal said. "And you'll either be starting a new and exciting life. Or you won't."

Ana had the feeling that if she had a choice, she'd definitely go with the new and exciting life. Mostly she just wanted her mom. She blinked away tears and sniffled once. She couldn't cry. Her nose always got completely stuffed up when she cried. And with tape over her mouth, she wouldn't be able to breathe.

To distract herself, she looked around the room, hoping to find something useful. She saw a pile of sealed cardboard cartons close by. She wondered if she could use the corner of a carton to peel the tape off her face.

Ana scooted closer. At first, Bryce resisted, giving her an annoyed grunt. Ana moaned and grunted back. Finally he scooted along with her until she was touching the boxes. She wiped her face against the corner over and over.

At first, it just made her face sore, but finally the tape caught on the box. Then she wiped more slowly, pressing her face into the corner. More and more of the tape rolled off, until Ana could talk.

"I did it," she said. "I can talk."

Bryce grunted in reply. While Ana had been scrubbing her face with the box, Bryce had been wiggling behind her. The wiggling was annoying, but she hoped it was part of some plan.

Suddenly, she felt a little more room between them near the bottom of the wrapped tape. Bryce continued to squirm. Ana pushed against the tape as well. Finally, Ana could move her arms. Then, she heard the rip of tape, and Bryce yelped, "Ow!"

"How did you get us loose?" Ana asked as she turned to look at him.

He grinned and held up a knife that had been thrown into one of the mats. "I went with my crazy idea earlier."

"Good," Ana said. "I'm feeling much better about crazy ideas."

Bryce quickly sliced through the tape on their ankles. They scrambled up and headed to the door. Ana just hoped they could figure out how to open it.

Just as they reached the door, it slid open on its own! They jumped back when they saw Connor in the doorway. "Come on," he said. "They're all together in the mission room talking about what to do with you two."

"So we should just trust you?" Bryce asked.

Ana put her hands on her hips and glared at Connor. "We tried to save you."

"I know," Connor said. "Once they caught us, I thought it would be better if they thought I was on their side. I was pretending."

Ana wasn't sure, but there wasn't time to argue. "Okay, get us out of here."

They raced down the hall and let themselves out at the front door. The buses were all gone out front, and Ana realized school must be out. They ran hard across the front lawn of the school. Then Ana stopped and pointed. "That's Officer Pat's car!"

They could all see the officer inside the car, reading something. "Do you think we should trust her?" Bryce asked.

"All the adults can't be in on this," Ana said. "I trust Officer Pat. She never yelled at us if we whispered or wiggled during her anti-bully presentation."

"Okay," Bryce agreed. Connor just nodded. They ran together and nearly plowed right into the door of her car. She climbed out, her eyes wide in surprise. She already knew that Ana and Bryce were missing. And she knew Connor had been missing for months. So convincing her that something crazy was happening at school wasn't too hard.

Connor told them everything. The principal and staff at Middlehurst Elementary School were really international criminals. They used the school as a hideout and even shipped stolen loot to themselves there.

Connor said that whenever they found a kid who was really good at the "special" activities like climbing or squeezing through tight spaces or rewiring security systems, the kid would disappear. Then the criminals would use the kid to help them commit their crimes.

Dozens of police officers searched the school. They found the criminals, the loot, and the poor kids who were locked up like Connor. The mayor gave Bryce and Ana a special award.

When it was all over, Ana was glad to go back to her regular life. She decided that sometimes it's okay to be a little bit adventurous. But only sometimes.

ENDING 2: FOGGY MEMORIES

Ana felt like cheering. She knew Connor wasn't really bad! "How do we get out?" she asked.

"There's another door through the office," Connor said.

"He's just trying to get us caught," Bryce insisted.

Ana didn't listen to him. She ran for the office door with Connor right beside her. She heard a frustrated huff from Bryce, but then he was pounding along behind them.

Connor jerked open the office door and they ran in. Behind the long office desk, the vice principal and the secretary were talking.

"Hey!" the secretary shouted. "Hold it right there!"

The kids didn't even pause. Connor ran past them and right through the principal's office door. Ana had never been in the principal's office, but she sure hoped Connor was right about a second door to outside.

As Ana raced into the principal's office, she skidded to a stop, her mouth hung open in shock. Her parents sat in chairs facing the principal's desk. A pretty blonde woman sat with them, and Ana assumed it must be Bryce's mom. The principal had lied about them leaving!

"Mom!" she yelled.

"Ana!" Her parents jumped to their feet and

hugged her. Then they both frowned at her. "I heard you were missing."

"Bryce," the blonde woman said, "what have you gotten into this time?"

"We've been here all along," Bryce said. "We found secret halls behind the walls. And we found some crazy training room where they practice throwing knives. And the principal tried to drag us back into the halls and punish us."

"Bryce," his mom's voice sounded sad, "it doesn't help if you make up stories."

"He's not!" Ana insisted. "It's all true. And we found Connor locked up in a room. So we were helping him escape when Principal Carson caught us."

Ana's father frowned. "Ana, this isn't like you."

"Children do disappoint us sometimes," Principal Carson said.

Ana spun and saw Principal Carson, Coach King, and the others from the main office had come into the room. Quickly each of them stepped up to one of the parents. They sprayed a mist into the parent's face.

The parents crumpled. They were caught by the other adults and eased back into their chairs.

"What did you do?" Ana demanded.

"We don't want to alarm your parents," Principal Carson said. "They are not hurt and should wake up right after we have our little chat."

"Chat?" Ana asked.

Principal Carson smiled and sat on the edge of his desk. Coach King walked over to stand in front of the door that Connor had told them about, the one that probably led outside. The secretary cast a nervous glance over the room, then hurried through the door to the outer office. The vice principal closed the door and stood in front of it.

"I guess we can chat," Bryce said.

"You behaved exactly as we expected," Principal Carson said. "We would have expelled you a long time ago if you hadn't shown so much skill at electrical wiring."

"What difference does that make?" Bryce asked.

"We have a rather special field of study here at Middlehurst Elementary School," Principal Carson said. "We train young operatives."

"Operatives?" Bryce echoed.

"Spies," Connor said.

The principal gave Connor a sharp look. "Operatives for certain agencies," he said. "Young people make perfect intelligence operatives. They so often go unnoticed."

"You want us to be spies?" Bryce said.

"No, I do not want you to be a spy," Principal Carson said. "Skills are not enough. You must be able to follow orders. Without that, you'd endanger every mission." He turned to Ana. "We had high hopes for you. Not only are you bright, you followed orders very well. Or you did until you met this young man."

Bryce smiled at that.

"So you wanted me to be a spy?" Ana said.

"We had hoped," the principal said. "You did well on early tests and we were preparing a special activity where Agent Connor would play a part. But you and your friend ruined that plan."

Ana turned to look at Connor. "So you weren't locked up?"

Connor shook his head. "No, I could come and go from that room. I was just resting and reading some training material." Then he smiled at her. "But I appreciate that you wanted to rescue me."

Principal Carson cleared his throat. "This is all top secret. Since neither of you is really right for our program, we'll have to erase your memory of today."

"I don't know," Connor said. "I still think Ana would be a great spy."

The principal snorted. Then he held up the spray he'd used on their parents and quickly sprayed Ana and Bryce in the face.

While Ana sat in the back of her parents' car for the drive home, she wondered if she'd ever live down the embarrassment. How could she have gotten herself locked in the janitor's closet all day with a boy? It's a good thing her parents were so nice about it.

Her mom turned in her seat to look back at Ana. "Why did you go into the closet with that boy in the first place?"

Ana opened her mouth to answer, then closed it. "You know, I don't remember."

Her parents both looked at one another and laughed.

Ana sat back in her seat and thought hard. Something about her mother's question bothered her. Why didn't she remember going into the closet? She thought about it until her head hurt. She was sure she'd remember eventually. She just knew it.

ENDING 3: FIRE!

"So now you're our friend again?" Ana asked. "What's going on with you?"

"I had to pretend to be on their side," Connor whispered. "Or they would have grabbed all three of us."

"What is this place?" Bryce demanded.

"I'll tell you everything," Connor promised. "But first we have to get somewhere safe."

Bryce crossed his arms and glared at Connor. "And where would that be?" he asked.

"Just trust me," Connor said.

"Right, because that worked so well last time," Bryce answered.

Ana knew they didn't have time to argue. She looked at the door leading outside. She really wanted to get out of there, but what if Connor was right? Then she spotted movement through the small window in the door. Someone was outside!

"Okay," she said, making a quick decision to trust Connor. "Get us out of here."

Connor took her hand and pulled her toward the office door. Ana almost pulled back. How could the school office be a safe place?

Ana and Connor ran into the office with Bryce right behind them. No one stood behind the long desk of the office. Connor half dragged Ana behind the desk and tugged on a painting that hung on the wall.

The painting tilted and the wall swung open. They hurried into the narrow, dark passage. Connor pulled the wall back into position, then he flipped a switch.

"Are you sure you should turn on the lights?" Ana asked.

"We don't have time to fall down," Connor said. "Hurry."

"You still haven't told us what's going on," Bryce said.

"It's an experiment," Connor said as he began moving quickly through the narrow hall. "The whole school is one big experiment. We're all test subjects."

"My parents wouldn't send me to a school like that," Ana said.

Connor glanced back at her. "You think someone asked them?"

"What kind of experiment?" Bryce asked. "I haven't had any lab tests done on me."

"They are experimenting on ways to make the perfect citizen," Connor said. "They are trying to create someone who is suspicious, observant, and always follows the rules."

"Why should we believe you?" Bryce asked.

Connor stopped so suddenly they almost ran over him in the narrow passageway. "I can show you. But you'll have to be quiet."

Ana and Bryce glanced at each other and then both nodded at Connor. They hurried through the passage for a while, then Connor stopped and slid open a small panel.

Connor pointed at it, silently telling Ana to look inside. Ana moved closer to take a look. She saw a classroom full of little kids with their heads on their desks. While they rested, a voice told them over and over to obey all rules and keep watch. The voice was soft, soothing, and very creepy.

Ana backed up, and Bryce took his turn looking in the room. When they were finished, Connor snapped the panel back.

"Kindergarten here has finger painting, counting, and brainwashing," he said.

"Okay, I believe you," Ana said. "But I haven't had any brainwashing classes since I've been here. We don't get nap time."

Connor looked at them. "Nap time isn't the only way they are getting to you. They put stuff in the lunches here," he said. "How come it doesn't work on you?"

"I bring my own lunch," Ana said. "I have food allergies."

Bryce shrugged. "The food tastes terrible so I always carry snacks." He pulled a granola bar, a small apple, and a slightly smashed box of raisins out of his pockets. "I don't eat much of it. And I really don't like rules."

Connor nodded. "It might not work on you. It doesn't on me. That's why they locked me up. They're trying to figure out how to make the medicine work on me, too."

"Why?" Ana said. "Why do any of this?"

"Principal Carson is in charge of it," Connor said. "I heard him say they were going to sell the program to the highest bidder once they proved it worked."

Ana looked sharply at Connor. "Wait, why were they throwing knives?"

"One of the things they want is citizens who aren't afraid of danger," Connor said. "Suspicion without fear. It's on a poster in one of the hidden rooms."

"So they were going to throw knives at us?" Bryce said, his voice loud.

"Shh! Do you want back in the program?" Connor snapped.

"Sorry," Bryce said. "So where's this safe place? How do we get out of here?"

"It's this way. It's not much farther," Connor said. They rushed through the passage until they reached a dead end. Then Connor pushed a lever and the end wall swung out. This time they were in the library behind a long shelf of books.

"We can get out the back door," Ana said, finally feeling like they might make it. They slipped carefully around the edges of the bookshelves to the door for the back hallway. The outside door wasn't far from there.

Connor put his ear to the hall door. He waited a moment, then gently opened the door and peeked out. He jerked his head back inside and pulled the door closed.

"The librarian is out there guarding the back door," Connor said. "We're stuck. I don't know of another way out."

"Wait," Bryce said. "Isn't there a fire alarm across the hall? The kind you just push?"

Connor glanced out the window. He looked back at Bryce and nodded.

Bryce smiled and pulled the apple out of his pocket again. "I played little league baseball at my last school. I think I can hit it."

Connor stepped away from the door and Bryce eased it open. He stood very still for a moment, then he threw the apple. Suddenly, the loud ringing of the fire alarm filled the school.

Ana cracked open the door and looked out. She saw the librarian race away down the hall. "Time to go," she said.

They were out the back door in moments. The fire alarm meant the whole school would empty out soon. The robo-students would stand in perfect lines until the principal gave the signal for everyone to return to their classes.

With that in mind, Ana, Bryce, and Connor ran as fast as they could across the open lawn. They had to reach the trees before the first teacher came outside.

Just before they vanished into the trees, Ana heard a yell behind them. They'd been discovered, but they had too much lead to be caught. Since Bryce lived closest, they ran to his house.

Bryce's mom called Ana and Connor's parents even before she had any idea what Bryce was talking about. Bryce grinned proudly as his mom made the calls. With all the parents finally together, the kids told their story.

Ana was surprised when the adults believed them almost right away. Even she had to admit their story was pretty wild. It helped that Connor was there, and he knew everything. His parents even cried when they saw him.

It took Connor most of the afternoon to finish his story. When he had told them everything, their parents called the police. By this time, school was over for the day.

Their parents convinced the police to search the school. When they did, they found all the stuff used for the experiment. They found boxes and boxes of research. Everything matched what Connor had described.

"Once we find Principal Carson and the teachers, they'll have a lot to answer for," the police detective told them.

Finding them proved to be the problem. Ana worried every day that Principal Carson and the others were just setting up a new experiment somewhere else. Finally, she got together with Connor and Bryce to make a video for the Internet. It went viral by the end of the day.

Pretty soon, almost everyone in the world had seen Ana's worried face looking out from their computer screen.

"My story is going to sound crazy, but I have to tell it," she began. "You have to know. You have to be careful. Don't let the experiment happen in your school . . . "

WRITE YOUR OWN ENDING

There were three endings to choose from in *A Really New School*. Did you find the ending you wanted from the story? Did you want something different to happen?

Now it is your turn! Write an ending you would like to happen for Ana, Connor, and Bryce. Be creative!